QREADS

BUS 99

TERI THOMAS

SADDLEBACK
EDUCATIONAL PUBLISHING

QREADS

SERIES 1
Black Widow Beauty
Danger on Ice
Empty Eyes
The Experiment
The Kula'i Street Knights
The Mystery Quilt
No Way to Run
The Ritual
The 75-Cent Son
The Very Bad Dream

SERIES 2
The Accuser
Ben Cody's Treasure
Blackout
The Eye of the Hurricane
The House on the Hill
Look to the Light
Ring of Fear
The Tiger Lily Code
Tug-of-War
The White Room

SERIES 3
The Bad Luck Play
Breaking Point
Death Grip
Fat Boy
No Exit
No Place Like Home
The Plot
Something Dreadful Down Below
Sounds of Terror
The Woman Who Loved a Ghost

SERIES 4
The Barge Ghost
Beasts
Blood and Basketball
Bus 99
The Dark Lady
Dimes to Dollars
Read My Lips
Ruby's Terrible Secret
Student Bodies
Tough Girl

SADDLEBACK
EDUCATIONAL PUBLISHING
www.sdlback.com

ISBN-13: 978-1-61651-214-9
ISBN-10: 1-61651-214-8
eBook: 978-1-60291-936-5

Printed in the U.S.A.
21 20 19 18 17   2 3 4 5 6

■ ■ ■

Waiting at the bus stop, Jamal Johnson was lost in his own thoughts. His long fingers fiddled with the straps of his backpack. A quiet young man of 22, Jamal was an art student at the local university.

He smiled as he thought of his mother, Letty. The bacon and eggs she'd fixed him that morning made him feel a little better. The tall, thin young man was tired. The night before, he'd crammed for an art history test until well after 1:00 A.M.

"A young man like you needs lots of protein," she'd declared. "The Lord knows you could use a lot more meat on those ribs, Jamal!" He laughed as she playfully poked him in the chest.

Jamal's older brother Luke was drinking coffee and reading the morning paper. He looked up with a grin and said, "What about me?"

"*You* don't need more protein, pal," Jamal teased. "With all your rippling muscles, you look like you *live* in the gym! Some people are just born lucky."

Luke never worked out, yet he had a near-perfect physique. Sometimes he tore the sleeves off his shirts just to show off his muscular arms. The tattoo on his left forearm—a heart, with "Mom" in the middle—looked good on his dark skin.

"Your father was big and strong like you, Luke," their mother said softly. "He always made me feel so safe." She wiped a tear from her eye.

■ ■ ■

Jamal felt a lump in his throat as he remembered what his mother had said. After eight years, she still missed his father so much.

Letitia—called Letty by her friends—was proud of both her sons. As a family, the three of them had pulled together to get through a terrible time.

The boys' father, Jake, an architect, had died in a car accident. He, Mom, and Jamal had been on their way to a sporting goods store to buy track shoes for Jamal. An 18-wheeler had run a red light, slamming into the driver's side of their car.

At the time, Jamal had been 14 and Luke, 16. Letty had been seven months pregnant. A few days after the accident, she'd lost the baby. Jamal, who'd been in the back seat, had gotten a deep gash over his left eye.

Now 22, Jamal was studying art. He was learning to design large architectural sculptures. Luke was a mechanic at a garage called Import Doctors. They serviced Jaguars, BMWs, Porsches, and Ferraris.

Friends sometimes teased Jamal and Luke about living at home with their mother. After all, they were single guys in their twenties! But living at home allowed them to save money. Luke dreamed of opening his own repair shop one day. And Jamal needed all of his money to pay for art supplies, books, and tuition.

But the real reason they still lived at home was their mother. Letty was still very sad sometimes. They couldn't bear to move out and leave her alone to struggle with her grief.

Ever since the accident, she'd had a very rough time. She had loved her husband so much! Losing both Jake and the baby so suddenly had been too much for her to bear. For a while, there were some days when she couldn't even get out of bed. Her lack of dependability had cost her several jobs.

These days, though, Letty was working regularly and starting to make some new friends. Her sons thought she seemed happier. Maybe the cloud was finally beginning to lift.

■ ■ ■

Jamal glanced at his watch. The bus should be there any minute.

His thoughts turned to the big architectural project his sculpture class was working on. A talented man named Nick Sanders was the professor in charge. Sanders had received a grant to build a towering sculpture for J&M, Inc., a giant corporation. The students in Jamal's class were excited. Under Sanders' supervision, they were being allowed to create the design and help oversee construction.

Once completed, the 30-foot-high, glass and steel structure would stand in front of J&M's office building. It would be the proud symbol of the company, which made machine parts. J&M would pay for the materials and the construction labor. Any money left over would go into the art students' scholarship fund.

The students had nearly finished the CAD (computer-aided design) drawings of the structure. When the company president approved the plans, construction would get started. It would take the better part of a year, or two semesters, to complete the project.

Jamal loved working with CAD. Like magic, it could show what a sculpture would look like before it was ever built. And, any part of the design could be changed with a few clicks of the mouse.

Jamal wondered what his father would have thought of CAD. He felt sorry for architects working in the old days before computers. What a waste of time to have to make drawings and blueprints by hand! At the time Jake Johnson had died, architects were only just beginning to use computers for drawing.

■ ■ ■

When the bus pulled up to the curb, Jamal reached down and grabbed his backpack.

A wiry guy in tight, electric-blue shorts

and a T-shirt was clamping a bicycle onto the front of the bus. A few people got off. Jamal stepped into the line of people crowding onto the bus.

He took a seat toward the back, where there was more room.

The ride to school usually took about 45 minutes. Jamal was grateful to have the time to cram for his art history test. He cracked open his book and tried to study.

Suddenly the driver slammed on the brakes. Some kind of commotion was going on outside, but Jamal couldn't tell what it was.

Then a man near the front spoke up. "I think it was a dog. Looks like he got out of the way just in time."

The bus started moving forward again. Jamal glanced out the window and saw a strange-looking little beast with a black and white spotted coat. *What in the world is that thing?* Jamal wondered. It looked a bit like an exotic monkey that might have escaped from the zoo.

The small creature was clutching some kind of shiny object. Then, suddenly, the creature raised its head and looked squarely at Jamal. An impish smile appeared on its face as it raised the shiny object. A bright flash from the object blinded Jamal for a moment. When he looked out the window again, the creature was gone.

Had that really happened? Jamal couldn't be sure. He looked around the bus, but no one else seemed to have noticed the incident.

He tried to go back to his book, but he couldn't concentrate. He just couldn't stop thinking about that weird little creature. *Just what was that thing? And what about that blinding light?* Jamal hoped it hadn't permanently damaged his eyes. Also, there now seemed to be a strange kind of low-level electricity crackling in the air inside the bus.

Again, Jamal looked around the bus. Several passengers were people he saw every day. They didn't seem any different. Everyone was reading, or looking out the window, or talking to other passengers. They acted like nothing out of the ordinary was happening. He glanced at the passing scenery, and it looked the same too.

Then Jamal blinked in surprise. Hank's News 'n' Views was on the wrong side of the street! On the way to school, the newsstand had always been on his left. Now it was on the right! Other businesses, though, were in the same places they'd always been.

Jamal began to feel uneasy. Was it possible that Hank had actually moved his newsstand across the street? Maybe he'd thought he'd sell more papers over there. The hard-working old guy was always trying to think of ways to make more money. Once he'd even tried handing out balloons that had *Hank's News 'n' Views* stamped on them. After a while, though, Hank had realized that the balloons were costing him too much money.

But to move the stand clear across the street? It would take a lot of people to do that. They'd have to tear down the stand, board by board, and rebuild it on the other side. Then they'd have to move all of the newspapers and magazines. And not only that, but all sorts of city permits would be required to make such a move.

Oh, for Pete's sake, Jamal scolded himself. *What's the big deal? People do crazy stuff like that all the time. Forget about it! Whatever Hank did was Hank's business.*

But then he saw something that made his heart leap into his throat.

■ ■ ■

The bus had stopped right in front of his favorite coffee shop. The neon sign in front had always said *The Meeting Place*. But today it said *The Meating Place*! How weird! Maybe the old sign had gotten damaged, and the workers had misspelled "Meeting" when they fixed it. But then Jamal noticed the artwork on the sign was a *leg of lamb*. The old artwork had been a big coffee mug with steam curling up from it.

Jamal had been coming to The Meeting

Place nearly every day after class. That's where he'd first met his girlfriend, Latonya. In fact, he'd arranged to study with her there this afternoon. But now the place was a *butcher shop* instead of a coffee shop?

"D-did you see that?" he sputtered to a woman sitting near him. He pointed at the sign. "That's s-supposed to be a *coffee* shop!"

"You must be from out of town," the woman smiled. "The word *Meating* is just a clever play on words. That butcher shop has been there for years."

The red awning, which said *Beef—Pork—Poultry,* had faded to a pinkish color. The white letters were cracked and peeling in some places. The awning looked like it had been there for a very long time.

Jamal panicked. At the next stop he hopped off the bus and took off running. He glanced over his shoulder as the bus pulled away. With a start, he noticed that it said *99* instead of 89! But there *was* no Bus 99! Jamal knew the city bus schedule by heart, so he was sure of that.

As he ran, Jamal tried to remember if he'd seen the bus's number when he got on. No—the guy clamping his bike to the front had been in the way. Jamal hadn't read the number. Still, the bus had been going the same direction as always. And the usual passengers on that route had been aboard.

It *had* to be the 89. So how come all of a sudden it said *99*? Had the city added a new bus? There had to be a reasonable explanation—didn't there?

■ ■ ■

Winded from sprinting eight blocks, Jamal stopped to catch his breath. He was standing in front of the shop where Luke worked.

As his breathing returned to normal, he looked up at the sign in front. Relieved, he saw that it was the same. Tall, neon letters spelled out *Import Doctors*. The picture showed a cartoon doctor holding a small red sportscar in his palm. His stethoscope was pressed against the side of the car, as if he were listening to its heartbeat.

Jamal rushed inside to look for Luke. He found his brother working under the hood of a sleek luxury car.

"Luke!" he cried out. "Man, am I glad to see you! And you don't even have green horns or anything!"

Then he realized Luke was working on a Lexus. It was a *Japanese* car! Import Doctors had always specialized in repairing only European cars. Glancing around, Jamal saw that every car in the place was Japanese! He sighed and shook his head. By now, he was starting to *expect* weird things to be happening out of the blue.

Luke looked concerned. "What's going on, Jamal?" he asked. "Aren't you supposed to be in class?"

"Oh, man, you won't believe this," Jamal burst out. "I can't believe it myself." Then he noticed Luke was wearing a gold wedding band. "You *are* still my brother, aren't you?"

"Last time I looked," Luke said. "Whassup? Are you losing it, bro?"

"Well," Jamal said, "I seem to have slipped into some kind of parallel universe. I know it sounds crazy. But first something darted in front of the bus. It almost got hit, but it scrambled out of the way just in time. Some guy thought it was a dog, but then it stopped by my window. It was one weird little critter, man! Then it looked straight at me, raised a shiny object it was holding, and blasted me right in the eyes! Luke, I couldn't see anything for a minute. I was, like, blind!"

"Okay, okay—calm down, Jamal!" Luke said. "I'm sure there's a reasonable explanation for all of this. You stayed up late studying last night, didn't you? I bet you fell asleep on the bus and had a bad dream."

"No, Luke. That's what I thought at first. But anyway—that was only the beginning!"

Then Jamal told Luke the rest of the story. He ended by asking when Import Doctors had suddenly started to service Japanese cars.

Now Luke was getting worried. He thought his brother must be cracking up.

He motioned for Jamal to sit down on a nearby chair.

"Let's see if you have a fever," he said, putting his hand on Jamal's forehead. "Hey, what's this? You've got a jagged scar above your left eye! I've never seen that before."

Jamal touched his forehead. Luke didn't know about the accident? Could it be? Had he stumbled into a universe where the car accident had never happened?

"I'm going to call Dad," Luke said. "He's just around the corner."

Jamal fainted.

■ ■ ■

When he came to, Jamal was stretched out in bed. His mother was leaning over him, looking worried.

"Oh, Mom, are you ever a sight for sore eyes," Jamal cried out. "You wouldn't believe all the weird stuff that happened to me today! I almost thought I'd been transported to a parallel universe. Luke was married, and Dad was still alive, and—"

Just then Jamal noticed the other people in the room. Luke was there, and his arm was around Latonya's waist. And Dad was standing next to them! He looked a little older, but it was him, all right. A little boy about eight stood right beside him.

Then Jamal looked closely at the tall, thin young man standing behind Dad. It was—*himself*!

"He looks just like me," the tall young man said. "The only difference I can see is the big scar over his left eye."

"Maybe he's an alien!" the little boy chimed in. "I bet he's one of those pod people! Boy, they did a great job of making him look just like my brother!"

Jamal was dumbstruck. *No—it couldn't be possible. Surely there was no such thing as a parallel universe. Or was there?*

"Okay, son," Dad said softly. "Why don't you just start at the beginning?"

"Sheesh, Dad! I just can't believe you're alive again," Jamal cried out. He reached out and touched his father's face. "It's amazing.

It's really you! And you're a normal, living, breathing, warm-blooded man. You sure don't look like a guy who's been *dead* for eight years. What's going on here?"

"You thought I *died*?" Dad asked. "Maybe I don't really want to know, son—but why don't you tell us the details. How did it happen?"

"There was a terrible car accident on August 8, 1996," Jamal said. "You, Mom, and I were on our way to buy me some track shoes. Luke had gone to a movie. An 18-wheeler ran a red light and plowed into the driver's side of our car. When I woke up, I was in the hospital. Mom told me you had died. It was terrible. A few days later, she lost the baby and—"

Shocked, Jamal stared at the boy.

"Is—is that my little brother?"

Jamal's mother was crying. She hugged the little boy fiercely. "Yes, son, this is Aaron," she said. "He was born on October 15, 1996."

The embarrassed boy struggled to get away from his mother. He was still fascinated by this stranger who looked just like his hero, Jamal.

"I remember that day," Mom said sadly. "We came *so* close to being hit broadside by that truck! Thank heaven Dad was able to swerve just in time."

"We were lucky," Dad said, picking up the story. "The truck did clip us and spin us around in the street. But no one was seriously hurt."

He looked at Jamal and spoke softly. "Well, young man, it seems that destiny has many paths. I'm so sorry that—in your world—your path took such a very sad turn."

■ ■ ■

The bewildering phenomenon still puzzled them all. But over the next few days, Jamal became great friends with the "other" Jamal. To tell them apart, the family was now calling the new Jamal by his middle name, Tyrone. It didn't matter that it was the *other* Jamal's middle name, too. It was just easier to call the new arrival Tyrone.

So that's what everybody did.

In this other universe, Jamal was an accounting student. He had his own apartment close to the university. Obviously, the family-with-a-father had a lot more money.

Tyrone told Jamal that he had once considered accounting. It had seemed like a solid career choice. After all, companies would always need someone to do payroll, taxes, and so on. But ever since Dad's death, Tyrone explained, architecture had seemed a lot more attractive. He'd always liked art, and the idea of carrying on his father's legacy appealed to him. So that's how he'd become an art student.

Mr. Johnson was proud that Tyrone was studying architectural sculpture. And he was interested in Tyrone's class project. The father and son had long talks about CAD, too. In this other universe, Dad used CAD all the time now. And, like Tyrone, Dad thought it was great—although he sometimes missed the old days of drawing by hand.

Tyrone was having a lot of fun with his

little brother, Aaron. The little boy loved playing basketball in the driveway with his lookalike brothers.

"You guys are *both* my heroes now!" Aaron exclaimed. "And Tyrone, I'm sorry about the 'pod people' putdown. You're just as cool as the *real* Jamal! I mean, uh—"

"I know what you mean, kiddo," Tyrone smiled, rubbing the boy's head. Then he scooped up his little brother and swung him around and around like an airplane. Aaron howled with glee.

Tyrone got to know his "other" mother, too. She had become a successful caterer. Several nights a week the *Letty's Catering* van brought heaping platters of home-cooked food to people's parties. Luke said she made great money at it and was very happy.

But Tyrone wished he could talk to his mother back home. He wanted to tell her that everything was fine—in a parallel universe. Dad hadn't died, and she'd never lost the baby. He wished she could see the strapping eight-year-old boy who loved to play basketball and watch science fiction movies. But he knew she'd never understand.

With a twinge of jealousy, Tyrone told Luke that, in his own universe, Latonya was *his* girlfriend—not Luke's wife. They'd met at The Meeting Place, a popular hangout with students. He explained that it was an Internet café as well as a coffee shop. For the price of a cup of coffee, you could use a computer there for 30 minutes.

Anyway, in *his* universe, that's how Tyrone and Latonya had met. He told Luke that he was crazy about her.

But in *this* universe The Meating Place was a butcher shop. So Tyrone was curious to know how Luke had met Latonya. Surely she hadn't been hanging out at the butcher shop!

"She came into the shop one time to get her Toyota fixed," Luke explained. "The U-joint was shot. I remember I was underneath an Acura at the time. All I could see was her pretty little feet and ankles. When I rolled myself out to talk to her, it was love at first sight."

Tyrone made a mental note. Once he got back to his own universe, he'd have to keep a closer eye on Luke. After all, Tyrone had met Latonya first. She was *his* girl.

■ ■ ■

The next day, Tyrone's dad pulled him aside. "Son, it's time for a family meeting. We have to find a way to get you back to your own home before long," he said. "Your mother must be worried sick by now."

Dad was right. He'd been away from home for nearly four days now! He could just imagine his mom and Luke reading the headlines:

YOUNG MAN ON BUS DISAPPEARS
STILL NO WORD ON MISSING YOUTH
POLICE SUSPECT FOUL PLAY

TV reporters would be at their house, shoving microphones and cameras into their faces. Mom would be crying and barely able to talk. Luke would be sick with worry, too. And so would Latonya.

"You're right, Dad," Tyrone said. "This whole business has been so mind-blowing that I forgot how hard this would be on Mom and Luke."

■ ■ ■

Aaron was the one to come up with the idea for getting Tyrone home. To him, it was simple. "Hey, it *had* to be that weird little creature—an alien, I bet—that sent you here. All you've got to do is find him and ask him to send you back."

That was easier said than done, of course. But no one had a better idea, so the worked out a plan. In an attempt to find the creature again, Tyrone would retrace his steps.

They put their scheme into action the next day. Tyrone put on the same clothes he'd been wearing when he arrived. He grabbed his backpack and walked into the living room, where the rest of the family was waiting. "Okay," he said in a shaky voice. "Let's do it!"

The whole family walked to the bus stop with Tyrone. "I—I don't know what to say," he stammered. "If this works, I'll never see you all again."

Dad reached out and pulled him into a great big bear hug. "Whatever happens, remember that we love you!" he said with a catch in his voice.

Then they heard the roar of an engine. Bus 99 was approaching. Dad stepped away from Jamal. "Goodbye, son. God bless."

■ ■ ■

Looking over his shoulder, Jamal smiled at his family one last time. Then, with mixed emotions, he stepped onto Bus 99. He walked down the aisle and took the same seat at the back of the bus. In a moment, the bus took off down the street.

Suddenly the driver slammed on the brakes. Some kind of commotion was going on outside, but he couldn't tell what it was.

Then a man near the front spoke up. "I think it was a dog. Looks like he got out of the way just in time."

The bus started moving forward again.

Jamal glanced out the window and saw a strange-looking little beast with a black and white spotted coat. . . .

"Oh, my God!" Jamal cried out. "It's actually happening again!"

He pressed his hands and face against the window, staring at the strange creature. "Please, please," he shouted, "send me home!"

The creature threw back its head and laughed. Jamal cringed at the mischievous cackle. Then the creature shrugged its shoulders and pointed the shiny object at Jamal.

Once again Jamal was blinded by the flash. Once again he could feel that strange electrical crackling in the air.

As the bus moved ahead, Jamal kept his head down, fearful of what he might see. Finally, he raised his eyes and looked at the bus number posted next to the driver—89! Then he looked out the window and saw The Meeting Place!

"Yahoo!" he shouted out.

■ ■ ■

Once again Jamal got off the bus at the next stop and ran the eight blocks to the Import Doctors shop. As he rushed in, he spotted Luke working on a Jaguar. And he wasn't wearing a wedding ring.

"Luke—Luke!" Jamal cried out. "I'm back!" He rushed over and grabbed his brother in a big hug.

Luke looked up. "Huh? Back from *where*, bro?" he laughed.

Jamal let go of his brother and stepped back. "What day is this, man?" he asked nervously.

"It's Monday," Luke said. "Are you all right, Jamal? What did you do—hit your head or something?"

Oh, wow! No time has passed here, Jamal thought. *Luke doesn't even know I've been gone. And if it's still Monday, I've got a test today!*

"Luke, the most amazing thing happened. I'll tell you about it tonight. You'll be blown away. But right now I have to get to class."

As Jamal rushed off to school, he wondered what—or *who*—that impish creature had been. Some kind of sicko alien that got its kicks by messing with people's lives? At this point he didn't care. Whatever it was, he was just glad it had brought him home!

■ ■ ■

The bus jolted to a stop. Jamal felt a hand on his shoulder, shaking him. "Hey, dude, wake up," a voice said. "This is your stop."

Jamal looked up into the smiling face of one of his classmates. As he picked up his backpack and stepped off the bus, he thought, *A dream—it had all been just a dream. . . .*

After-Reading Wrap-Up

1. There are many *genres,* or types, of fiction, such as adventure, detective, horror, etc. To what genre do you think *Bus 99* belongs? Explain your reasoning.

2. When Jamal and Luke were teenagers, a pivotal event changed their family. What was the event? What effect did it have on their mother?

3. What strange being did the author create to trigger Jamal's passage to and from a parallel universe? Describe a different device that might have been used to trigger the same effect.

4. How did Latonya's relationship to each brother change from one universe to the other?

5. List three important changes that made Letty's life much happier in the parallel universe.

6. Think about the end of the story. Suppose Jamal had *not* been dreaming. Explain your idea for a different ending.